# Chapter One

Dad was at work. Grandma was reading in the garden. Mum had gone to help her friends at the retirement centre. Manju was bored.

"Let's do something fun," said Manju to Cumin, her cat.

"Miaow!" Cumin agreed.

"Maybe we can make a wish," said Manju. "MIAOW!" Cumin warned. *That doesn't sound like a good idea*, he thought.

Last time they made a wish, the genie had brought snotty aliens, a loud rock band, naughty giants and curious fairies.

But Manju had already opened the cupboard in Grandma's room. She picked up the lamp and remembered Grandma's instructions.

Step 1: Put on a smile.
Step 2: Rub the sides of the lamp three times.
Step 3: Whisper the magic words: *"Jantar Mantar Jeeboomba!"*

The window closed. The room darkened and a whiff of rainbow smoke rose from the lamp.

Cumin hid under the bed and watched. When the smoke cleared, the genie stood in front of them.

"Hello," said Manju. "Greetings to you."

"Aaaachooo!"

# Chapter Two

"Are you ill?" asked Manju.

"I've got a terrible cold," said the genie.

"Did you drink some hot tea?" asked
Manju. "That's what Grandma does."

"No time for that," said the genie. "Too
many lamps are being rubbed. What
did you summon me for?"

"It's so quiet in here," said Manju. "I want excitement."

"Hurry up then," said the genie, pulling his shawl tighter around his shoulders. "Make a wish."

Manju closed her eyes and thought about it for a moment.

Cumin purred. *Be careful what you wish for*, he thought.

"I wish for a water slide," said Manju.

"Whatever for?" asked the genie. "That's the strangest thing anyone has ever asked me."

Manju didn't think water slides were strange. Until…

# Chapter Three

… A big slide appeared in the room. And squealing otters came sliding down it. "MIAOW!" Cumin snarled from under the bed.

"Genie, what have you done?" asked
Manju.
"Didn't you wish for an otter slide?"
asked the genie.
"NO!"

Oh dear! The genie sat sadly on the
bed, shaking his head. He blew his nose
hard. "BLEEEEEURGH!"
"Are you ok?" asked Manju.
The genie blew again!

"BLEEEEEURGH!"

"This cold has blocked me up," he said.
"I can't hear properly."
"SQUEAL!" The otters came sliding
down the slide.

"Genie!" said Manju gently. "Please would you make the otters go away?"

"They're already grey," said the genie. "Aren't they?"

Manju shouted, "I wish you would make the otters go away!"

"Thanks for shouting!" said the genie, clicking his fingers. The otters vanished.

# Chapter Four

"I've messed up twice already," said the genie, sobbing. "Before I came here, I conjured up blue goats."

"Why?"

"A boy asked for a boat," replied the genie. "... I think."

Cumin snorted, thinking about angry blue goats.

"One more mistake," said the genie, "and I'll be struck off the Genie Register. Forever!"

"Sorry I called you," said Manju. "Maybe I should have done something on my own, when I was bored."

Cumin huddled on Manju's lap. He felt sorry for the genie too.

"TRRRRRRNNNNNNG!"
Manju looked around.
"TRRRRRRRNNNNNNG!"
Cumin looked around.
The genie didn't look. He was fast asleep.

"TRRRRRRNNNNNG!"

"Genie, wake up!" said Manju. "I think you are being summoned." Startled, the genie checked his Genie-O-Summoner.

"This is not good," he said. "I've got to go."

"Bye," said Manju. "Take care."

WHOOSH!

# Chapter Five

As the genie disappeared, Manju was lifted up too. Uh oh! She must have been sitting on his shawl.

Cumin clung on to Manju tightly. *Cats are not meant to fly*, he thought.

**WHOOSH!**

In a swirl of rainbow haze and sparkling fog, the genie whooshed along. But his sneezing made the ride quite bumpy. "Maybe we're going to a magical kingdom," whispered Manju. "Or to a pirate ship with girl pirates."

*I'd make a great pirate cat*, thought Cumin. BUMP!

The fog cleared. It wasn't a kingdom or a pirate ship. They were inside a room at the retirement centre.

"Hello, Genie," said a voice. "My name is Mrs Rose Cox."
"Aaachooo!" replied the genie. "Hello Mrs Close Fox!"
"Miaow!" Cumin hid behind Manju. This wasn't going well at all.

# Chapter Six

Manju stepped out from behind the
genie. "Hello Mrs Cox," said Manju.
"Genie isn't feeling well today."
"Oh bless him," she said.
"I can do that," said the genie, clicking
his fingers.
A chess set appeared on the table.
Mrs Cox gasped.

"Did you wish for something else?" asked the genie. He began to cry. "Did I mess up a third time?"

"No, no, Genie," she said. "This is exactly what I wanted."

Cumin snorted. *Of course not*, he thought. Genie slumped down on the sofa and closed his eyes.

"MIAOW!" *How about some milk,* thought Cumin. Genie clicked his fingers without opening his eyes. A soft silk cloth fell on top of Cumin. Cumin purred. Some mistakes were soft.

Mrs Cox sat at the table.
She touched the chess pieces.
"These are beautiful," she said.
Manju sat opposite to her.

"Mrs Cox, why did you call the genie?"
asked Manju. "I know you didn't want
the chess set."

"I was bored," said Mrs Cox.

"Me too," said Manju.

"Grandma taught me how to play chess,"
she said. "Would you like to play?"

"What a fabulous idea," said Mrs Cox. While they played chess, the genie slept on the sofa. Cumin lay on his belly going up and down, under the silk.

# Chapter Seven

Manju and Mrs Cox were on their third game. Manju had won the first game. Mrs Cox had won the second. The final game looked too close to call.

"MIAOW!" called Cumin. It was time for his milk.

"Shh!" said Manju. "I need to concentrate. Suddenly a bowl of milk appeared in front of Cumin.

Cumin turned to look at the genie. The genie winked and put a finger to his lips. "Shh!"

Manju moved her pawn two steps forward.

"Yes!" cried Mrs Cox, moving her king. "Check!"

Manju was waiting for this moment. She moved a piece. She cried, "CHECK MATE!"

Game over! Manju had won.
"Well done," said Mrs Cox.
DING-DING-DING-DING! The
clock chimed.
"Oh my!" said Mrs Cox. "It's time for
my tea, biscuits and dance practice."
The genie's job was done. In a whiff
of rainbow smoke and sparkly
fog, he disappeared.

And right on cue, the door opened.
"What are you doing here?" asked
Manju.
"What are YOU doing here?" asked
Mum. She was carrying a pot of tea
and a plate of biscuits.

# Chapter Eight

Manju told Mum everything – about the genie and his cold, the otter slide and how they flew with the genie. "Mmm," Cumin purred. He wanted to tell everyone about the silk and the milk. But he was too cosy to get up.

"It's very nice that you helped Genie,"
said Mum. "And kept Mrs Cox company."
"I enjoyed playing chess," said Mrs Cox.
"And I'm not bored anymore," said Manju.
"Maybe you can visit every week to play,"
said Mum.
"We'd like that," said Mrs Cox and
Manju together.

"I hope Grandma isn't worried," said
Mum, as they walked back to the car.
"I hope Genie feels better soon,"
said Manju.
"Me too," said Mum, carrying Cumin.
"MIAOW!" Cumin agreed.

PILLGWENLLY
13-10-21